Put Beginning Readers on the Right Track with
ALL ABOARD READING™

The All Aboard Reading series is especially designed for beginning readers. Written by noted authors and illustrated in full color, these are books that children really want to read—books to excite their imagination, expand their interests, make them laugh, and support their feelings. With fiction and nonfiction stories that are high interest and curriculum-related, All Aboard Reading books offer something for every young reader. And with four different reading levels, the All Aboard Reading series lets you choose which books are most appropriate for your children and their growing abilities.

Picture Readers
Picture Readers have super-simple texts, with many nouns appearing as rebus pictures. At the end of each book are 24 flash cards—on one side is a rebus picture; on the other side is the written-out word.

Station Stop 1
Station Stop 1 books are best for children who have just begun to read. Simple words and big type make these early reading experiences more comfortable. Picture clues help children to figure out the words on the page. Lots of repetition throughout the text helps children to predict the next word or phrase—an essential step in developing word recognition.

Station Stop 2
Station Stop 2 books are written specifically for children who are reading with help. Short sentences make it easier for early readers to understand what they are reading. Simple plots and simple dialogue help children with reading comprehension.

Station Stop 3
Station Stop 3 books are perfect for children who are reading alone. With longer text and harder words, these books appeal to children who have mastered basic reading skills. More complex stories captivate children who are ready for more challenging books.

In addition to All Aboard Reading books, look for All Aboard Math Readers™ (fiction stories that teach math concepts children are learning in school); All Aboard Science Readers™ (nonfiction books that explore the most fascinating science topics in age-appropriate language); All Aboard Poetry Readers™ (funny, rhyming poems for readers of all levels); and All Aboard Mystery Readers™ (puzzling tales where children piece together evidence with the characters).

All Aboard for happy reading!

To my Aunt Jet – Godmother
and Giver of Books—J.M.M.

For my little ones, Oliver and Harper—B.L.

GROSSET & DUNLAP
Published by the Penguin Group
Penguin Group (USA) Inc., 375 Hudson Street, New York, New York 10014, USA
Penguin Group (Canada), 90 Eglinton Avenue East, Suite 700,
Toronto, Ontario M4P 2Y3, Canada
(a division of Pearson Penguin Canada Inc.)
Penguin Books Ltd., 80 Strand, London WC2R 0RL, England
Penguin Group Ireland, 25 St. Stephen's Green, Dublin 2, Ireland
(a division of Penguin Books Ltd.)
Penguin Group (Australia), 250 Camberwell Road,
Camberwell, Victoria 3124, Australia
(a division of Pearson Australia Group Pty. Ltd.)
Penguin Books India Pvt. Ltd., 11 Community Centre, Panchsheel Park,
New Delhi—110 017, India
Penguin Group (NZ), 67 Apollo Drive, Rosedale, North Shore 0632, New Zealand
(a division of Pearson New Zealand Ltd.)
Penguin Books (South Africa) (Pty.) Ltd., 24 Sturdee Avenue,
Rosebank, Johannesburg 2196, South Africa

Penguin Books Ltd., Registered Offices:
80 Strand, London WC2R 0RL, England

Illustrations by Bryan Langdo.

Text copyright © 2010 by Jean M. Malone. Illustrations copyright © 2010 by Penguin Group
(USA) Inc. All rights reserved. Published by Grosset & Dunlap, a division of Penguin Young
Readers Group, 345 Hudson Street, New York, New York 10014. ALL ABOARD READING and
GROSSET & DUNLAP are trademarks of Penguin Group (USA) Inc. Printed in the U.S.A.

Library of Congress Control Number: 2009015127

ISBN 978-0-448-45265-4   10 9 8 7 6 5 4 3 2

The Miracle of Easter

By Jean M. Malone
Illustrated by Bryan Langdo

Grosset & Dunlap

An Imprint of Penguin Group (USA) Inc.

In the spring,
trees grow new leaves.
Baby birds hatch
and flowers bloom.
Springtime is a season
of new life and hope.

Every spring, there is

a special holiday.

It can be in March or April,

but it is always on a Sunday.

Do you know what day it is?

It's Easter, of course!

Easter is an important

Christian holiday.

Just like spring,

Easter is about new life and hope.

That is because it celebrates the day

when Jesus rose from death to new life.

Before Jesus died,

no one could go to Heaven.

Jesus changed all that

on the first Easter.

Jesus is God's Son.

God loves us very much,

so He sent His only Son

to save us from our sins.

Sins are all the bad and mean
things that people do.

Most of the time people are good.

But everyone makes mistakes.

Jesus lived a long time ago
in the land of Nazareth (say: NAH-zuh-reth).
He was a carpenter (say: CAR-pin-tur).
Carpenters build things out of wood,
like benches and tables.

Jesus was also a great teacher.

People came from miles around

to hear His parables (say: PAIR-uh-bulls).

A parable is a story that teaches a lesson.

Jesus also made miracles.

He healed the sick.

He made the blind see.

Jesus even walked on water.

Once, He calmed the stormy sea

just by telling it, "Be still."

The people loved Jesus.

They thought He

was a prophet (say: PRAH-fit).

That means they believed

that when Jesus spoke,

He was saying God's words.

They didn't know that
He was God's Son.
But they knew that
He was special.

Not everyone loved Jesus, though.
The rulers of the land
were jealous (say: JELL-us) of Him.
They thought the people loved Jesus
more than they loved the rulers.

The rulers believed Jesus was turning the people against them.
But that wasn't true.

Jesus had 12 close friends
called disciples (say: di-SIGH-pulls).
They followed Jesus everywhere.

One disciple was named Judas.

He was very foolish and greedy.

The jealous rulers wanted

to get rid of Jesus.

They needed help,

so they went to Judas.

They told him that they
would pay him 30 silver coins
if he would help their soldiers
arrest Jesus.

Greedy Judas said, "Yes."

Because Jesus is the Son of God,

He knew what was in Judas's heart.

He knew what Judas planned to do.

Even though Judas was a sinner,

Jesus still loved him.

Jesus forgave Judas for his greed.

One night, Jesus and His friends
ate a big feast together.
Judas was there, too.
Today, we call this
the Last Supper.

Before dinner, Jesus washed
His disciples' feet.
In that time, people always wore sandals,
and they walked everywhere
on dusty roads.
Their feet got very dirty.

Jesus washed His friends' feet
to show them
that they should treat people
with kindness—
just as He was doing.

Then Jesus tried to warn His friends
about what was going to happen to Him.
Jesus told them that soon
He would not be with them.

He had to go so that
He could make a place
for them in Heaven,
with his Father.
Jesus said not to be scared,
because He would come
back to visit them.

Jesus gave His friends

bread and wine.

He told them,

"Eat this and remember me."

The disciples didn't understand,

but they did what Jesus said.

After dinner, Jesus went

to a garden to pray

with some of His disciples.

The rulers sent their soldiers

into the garden.

Then Judas kissed Jesus on the cheek.

The kiss was a signal

for the soldiers to arrest Jesus.

They said Jesus

had broken the law,

even though He had not.

The soldiers took Jesus to court.

The judge was named Pilate (say: PIE-lit).

He felt sorry for Jesus.

Pilate asked Jesus,

"Are you the Son of God?"

Jesus answered, "Yes."

No one understood

how that could be true.

They thought Jesus must be lying.

Pilate wanted to let Jesus go,

but he gave in to the rulers.

He let the soldiers take Jesus away

to punish Him.

At the top of a hill,

the soldiers put Jesus on a cross.

Even though they had hurt Him,

Jesus forgave the soldiers.

He forgave Judas and

the rulers and Pilate, too.

Jesus prayed, "Father, forgive them.

They do not know

what they are doing."

Then He died.

The disciples buried Jesus
in a tomb (say: TOOM),
which was like a cave.
They pushed a heavy stone
in front to block the door.

Three days later, some women
went to visit Jesus's tomb.
When they got there,
the women were amazed.
The big, heavy stone
had been moved away!

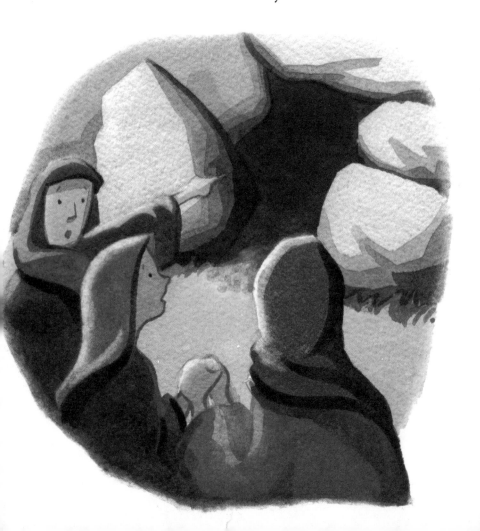

The women went inside.

Jesus was gone.

The women were very upset.

Then they saw an angel
waiting for them.
The angel said that Jesus
had risen from the dead!
He was going to Heaven
to be with God,
just like He had promised.

The women were very happy

when they heard the angel's news.

They ran all the way home

to tell the disciples.

They said, "Jesus is not dead!

He has risen to new life!"

The day when Jesus rose to new life
was the very first Easter Sunday.

Dying on the cross

and rising on Easter

was Jesus's greatest miracle.

When He died, Jesus took away

the people's sins

so they could be saved

and go to Heaven, too.

Every spring on Easter Sunday,
many families go to church.
They pray, sing songs, and rejoice.
They thank Jesus for the precious
gifts He gave them—
the gifts of new life and new hope.